LIBRARY MOUSE
MOUSE
A Friend's Tale

DANIEL KIRK

Abrams Books for Young Readers
New York

For Frederick, and all of the children
who write and illustrate their own little books
—D.K.

Author's Note:
It's the perfect combination of words and pictures that makes a book we want to read again and again. Many of our favorite picture books and early readers were created by author-and-illustrator partners. Sometimes an author and illustrator work together, face-to-face, and sometimes, like Sam and Tom, they never even meet! The fact remains that the stories we love just wouldn't be the same if the writer or illustrator were replaced by someone else. That's how important the right combination is. The magic they make together is greater than the sum of its parts.

Since my book *A Friend's Tale* is about "how teamwork can make a great book," as Mrs. Forrester, the librarian, says, I thought it would be fun to put some of the great collaborators of children's books in the backgrounds of my own illustrations. I asked some of my librarian friends for suggestions about the author-illustrator partners who are important to them and to the children they spend time with every day.

I wish to thank the following librarians for their suggestions: Heidi Cadmus, Laura-lee Foerster, Judith Gantly, Miriam Ghabour, Susan Koenig, Starr Latronica, and Linda Simpfendorfer.

Library of Congress Cataloging-in-Publication Data

Kirk, Daniel.
Library mouse : a friend's tale / written and illustrated by Daniel Kirk.
p. cm.
Summary: Sam, the shy mouse that lives in the library and likes to write books, collaborates with a boy in the library's Writers and Illustrators Club.
ISBN 978-0-8109-8927-6
[1. Libraries—Fiction. 2. Authorship—Fiction. 3. Mice—Fiction. 4. Bashfulness—Fiction.] I. Title.

PZ7.K6339Lib 2009
[E]—dc22
2008024686

Book design by Chad W. Beckerman

Printed and bound in China
10 9 8 7 6 5 4 3 2 1

Abrams Books for Young Readers are available at special discounts when purchased in quantity for premiums and promotions as well as fundraising or educational use. Special editions can also be created to specification. For details, contact specialmarkets@hnabooks.com or the address below.

HNA
harry n. abrams, inc.
a subsidiary of La Martinière Groupe

115 West 18th Street
New York, NY 10011
www.hnabooks.com

SAM WAS A LIBRARY MOUSE. He lived in a little hole
in the wall behind the children's reference books. Sam
loved to read, and he loved to write, too. Everyone loved
his little books. But Sam was very shy, and no one at
the library had ever met him.

Once a week, the children at the library met for Writers and Illustrators Club.

"For our next project," said Mrs. Forrester, the librarian, "I would like all of the boys and girls to work with a partner. One of you will be the author, and the other will be the illustrator. You will find out how teamwork can make a great book!"

At the end of the meeting, there was one child left standing by himself. "Don't worry, Tom," said Mrs. Forrester. "I'd be happy to work with you!"

When night came, Sam the library mouse went to do some research for a story he was planning to write. All night long, he studied, jotting down things in his notebook. But as the sun rose, his eyelids grew heavy and he fell asleep.

Squeak! Sam awoke with a start as children filed into the room. In his hurry to escape, he left his little notebook behind! Tom discovered it on the librarian's desk. Carefully, he opened the cover and turned the pages. Then he went to tug at Mrs. Forrester's sleeve.

"What's this?" said the librarian, flipping through the notebook. "From the titles of the stories in here, I would guess this belongs to Sam, our mystery author. He's written so many books, and yet we've never had the pleasure of meeting him!"

"Let's put it back on your desk," said Tom, "so Sam will find it!"

That night, Sam climbed onto the librarian's desk to look for his notebook. As he hurried back across the desk with his prize in his arms, the mouse stepped across an ink pad and left behind a trail of footprints.

"Good morning," Mrs. Forrester said to Tom when he arrived early the next day. "Did you bring some ideas for a story we can work on together?"

"Not yet," said Tom. Then he noticed the inky marks on the librarian's desk, and saw that Sam's notebook was gone. "Impossible," he thought.

When he was sure no one was looking, Tom got down on his hands and knees. He peered beneath the library shelves and around the baseboards, not quite certain what he was looking for. Suddenly, he saw a little hole in the wall. Now he knew why Sam always seemed to write about mice!

Tom tore a piece of cheese from the snack he had brought, and he left it by the opening.

"Oh, no!" Sam cried when he stepped out of his hole that night and saw the cheese. "Who could have left it?" he wondered. "What do they want?" Sam thought it might be best to leave the cheese alone and pretend he had never seen it.

The next time Tom came to the library, he found the cheese, looking dry and lonely, just where he had left it. He replaced it with a peanut butter cracker. "Maybe Sam will like this better," he thought. Indeed, when Sam awoke and smelled the cracker, it was all he could do not to gobble up the treat. Clearly, someone had discovered his hole. Sam hoped that if he ignored the food, whoever it was would go away and forget about him!

But Tom did not forget about Sam. He thought about writing a letter to the library mouse, but he wasn't sure what to say. Then he got an idea. He sat down and started to write a story. It was called *The Shy One*, and this is how it began:

"Once upon a time, there was someone who was very shy. His name was Sam. People seemed to make him nervous. The children at the library knew what Sam was like, because of the books he wrote. But nobody really knew who Sam was, and that seemed to suit him just fine. Until one day . . ."

When he finished writing, Tom folded up the paper and left it just outside the little hole in the wall.

That night, Sam read the story from beginning to end. Tom had discovered the one thing Sam could not resist: a story! Sam grinned. He remembered Tom as a regular at the library. "I've got an idea," he said to himself, then went into his hole and got to work.

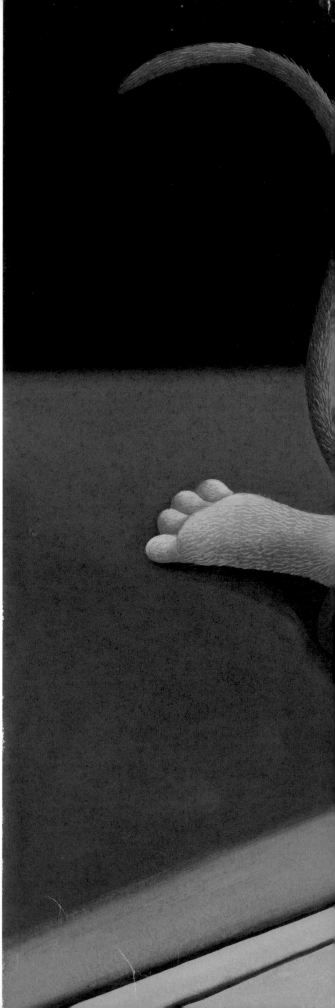

When Tom arrived later that week for Writers and Illustrators Club, he felt a little guilty. He'd been so busy thinking about Sam that he'd forgotten to do his assignment! He got down on his hands and knees to look beneath the reference books. The paper he had left there was gone. Then he heard the librarian's voice. "Tom, what's this I found on my desk? I thought you'd decided not to work on a book this week, and then I found *The Shy One*, written by you and illustrated by Sam! I can't wait to share it with the group!"

"Oh, no!" thought Tom. The story he had written had been meant just for Sam to see. What if Sam had drawn a boy and a mouse? If Mrs. Forrester read it out loud, everyone would find out who Sam really was, and then what? Someone might try to hurt him or chase him away. "Please don't read the story, Mrs. Forrester," Tom pleaded.

"You should be proud of your work," the librarian said kindly. "And how wonderful that you did a book together! I can't wait to hear more about who Sam really is!"

In this, Tom and Sam's first book together, they discover the rewards of friendship and teamwork!

the SHY one

written by Tom
illustrated by Sam

When everyone was seated, Mrs. Forrester held up the little book. She began to read:

"Once upon a time, there was someone who was very shy. His name was Sam. People seemed to make him nervous. The children at the library knew what Sam was like, because of the books he wrote. But nobody really knew who Sam was, and that seemed to suit him just fine. Until one day someone discovered Sam's secret. It was a good thing he only wanted to be Sam's friend . . ."

Mrs. Forrester read the story from beginning to end, and Tom was amazed to see the pictures that Sam had drawn. The illustrations showed two mice instead of one, and one of them was named Tom!

"So tell us," said Mrs. Forrester, "just who is this Sam who writes so many of our books? I just have to ask: Is it you?"

"Oh, no," answered Tom, with a shy smile. "I just wrote the story. Sam is real. But he likes his privacy, so that's all I'm going to say! A friend knows how to keep a secret."

When the library was ready to
close, and Tom was sure that no
one was watching, he bent to place
something on the floor beneath the
children's reference books. Sam
awoke that night to find a note
outside his hole.

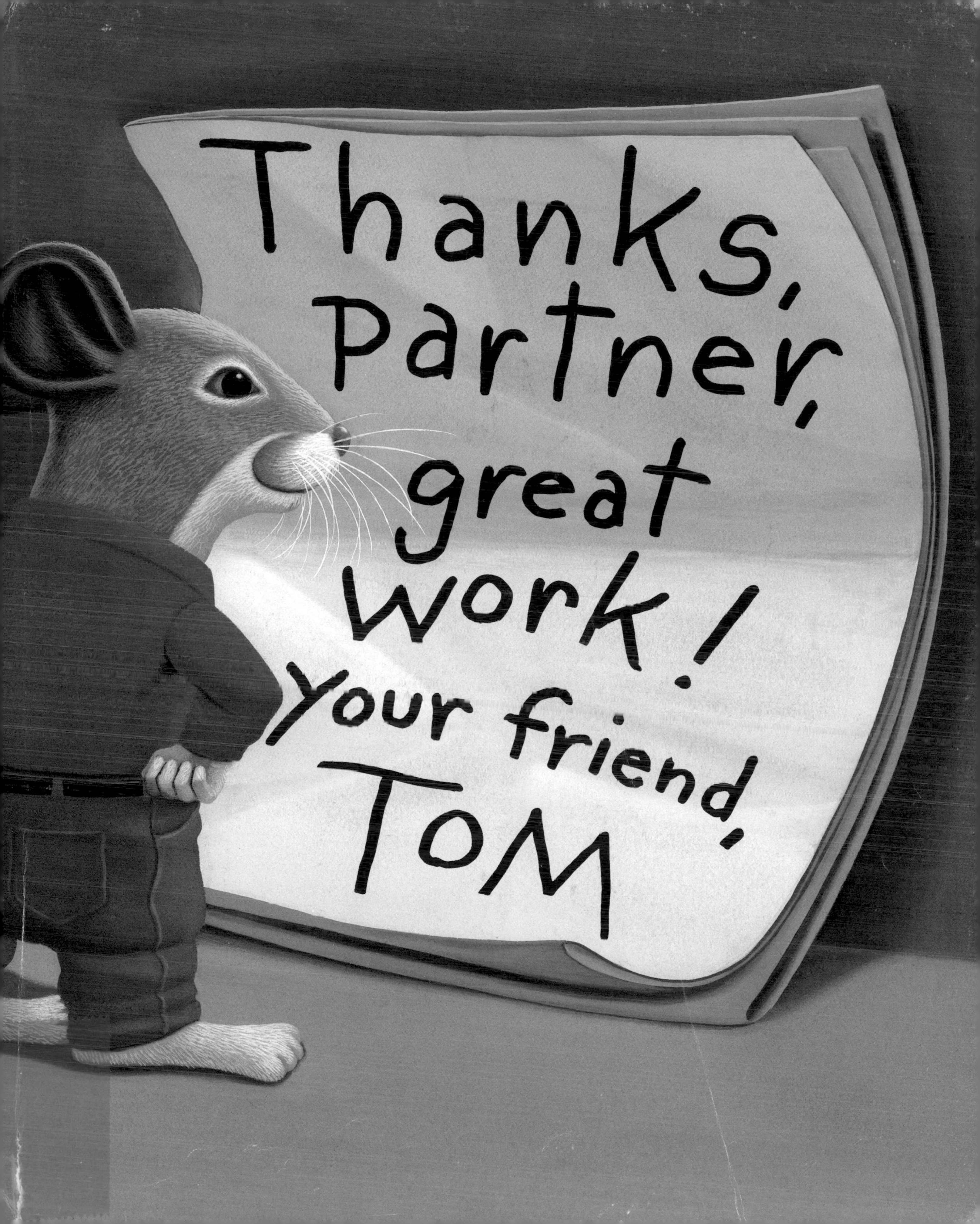
Thanks,
Partner,
great
work!
Your friend,
TOM

Sam sat down at his desk. He had an idea for his own story about friends. He couldn't wait for Tom to read it! And maybe this time, his new friend would draw the pictures.

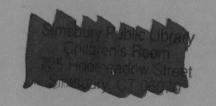